BURNING FLAME

N. Viktoria

N. Viktoria/Alphazuriel Publishing
United States

Cover © 2022 Anchorage

Burning Flame/ N.Viktoria -- 1st ed.
ISBN 9798371328885

CONTENTS

Ava was a tall, and curvy black woman in her mid-thirties. She had dark skin, a beautiful face, and long, wavy hair that she kept in a tight ponytail.

Ava had never been much for bars, but her friend had convinced her to come here tonight.

As she walked into the crowded bar, Ava couldn't help but feel a little out of place. She had never been one for crowded, noisy places, and she had only come to this particular bar because her friend had insisted on it.

But as she scanned the room, her eyes landed on a tall, handsome man standing at the bar. He had dark, curly hair and a chiseled jawline, and Ava felt an immediate attraction to him.

She hesitated for a moment, wondering if she should go talk to him. But before she could make a decision, he turned and caught her eye.

"Hi there," he said, approaching her with a friendly smile. "I'm Mason."

"Hi, I'm Ava," she replied, feeling her pulse race.

As they made small talk, Ava found herself getting lost in Mason's deep, dark eyes. She couldn't believe how attracted she was to him, and she knew that she had to see him again.

The next day, Ava went back to the same bar, hoping to run into Mason. When she spotted him waiting at the bar, she didn't hesitate to walk up to him.

"Hey!" he exclaimed when she approached. "What are you doing here?"

He wrapped his arms around her waist from behind and gave her a kiss on the cheek. His lips were soft and warm, and Ava felt herself melting against him. As they shared another long, passionate kiss, she ran her hand down the front of his chest and through the short hairs on his neck. She gasped softly as she felt a bead of sweat trickle down between her breasts.

As their tongues continued exploring each other's mouths, Ava moaned loudly and pressed her body even more tightly into Mason's. He leaned into her with an intense hunger that excited her. He pulled away slightly and looked deeply into her eyes, then reached and touched her breasts. Her breathing became ragged and shallow, and she shuddered with pleasure.

They quickly found themselves in a private booth in the back corner of the bar, making out passionately. Mason grabbed her shirt by the collar and began undoing its buttons while she fumbled with his pants. When she finally got them unbuttoned, he peeled away Ava's tight-fitting dress.

As Ava let out a low moan, Mason gently bit down on one of her nipples and sucked on it. Then he moved his mouth lower and pushed aside Ava's underwear to reveal her shaved pussy. She trembled beneath him as he ran his tongue along her slit before diving inside. She felt waves of ecstasy radiate outward from where his tongue was moving inside her, and all the strength left her legs until she collapsed onto the floor beside the table.

CHAPTER TWO

Ava and Mason hit it off immediately, and they soon found themselves on a second date. This time, they went to a cozy little Italian restaurant, and Ava was thrilled to have the chance to get to know Mason better.

As they talked and laughed over a bottle of wine, Ava couldn't believe how easy it was to be with Mason. He was charming, intelligent, and handsome, and she felt herself falling for him more and more with each passing moment.

As the night came to an end, Mason walked Ava to her door and hesitated for a moment before leaning in to kiss her. Ava melted into the kiss, feeling a spark ignite between them. They stood outside her door for a long moment kissing softly against her closed front door, then made their way upstairs together.

Once again, Mason undressed Ava, slowly pulling away her clothing as their kisses continued. As he laid her naked body down on her bed, he ran his fingers through her pubic hair, then bent his head down and began sucking on one of her nipples while his hands explored every inch of her body. His touch sent shivers down her spine, and Ava moaned and writhed beneath him. She held his face firmly in her hands and kissed him deeply, enjoying every sensation she could feel from his lips and tongue exploring her body. Then she pulled him up so that she could guide him towards the spot deep within her that she had been craving since the first day they met.

As Mason slid inside her wet pussy, she let out another loud moan and wrapped her legs around his back to pull him even closer. When he started moving inside her, it felt like heaven. The feelings were almost too much, but Ava loved how intense everything was.

Ava and Mason stayed together for the next two days, making love non-stop. He always made sure to give Ava pleasure before giving himself any, which made Ava want to please him more than ever. After spending so many nights sleeping alone, she really wanted to spend the rest of her life with Mason.

On Saturday night, as she got ready for work, she decided not to wear a bra under her top. She thought that she looked very sexy when her breasts jiggled slightly underneath her white button-down shirt. And it wasn't just her chest that drew attention—her whole body seemed to shine in the light of the candle that lit up her bathroom counter.

When she arrived at work, Ava found herself flirting shamelessly with everyone she saw. Her coworkers all knew about Ava's secret romance and couldn't stop asking questions about her new man. Some even gave Ava advice on how to keep her relationship strong, saying things like "Don't make him choose" or "Give him what he wants."

As Ava made her way home after closing on Sunday evening, she could hardly contain her excitement over seeing Mason again.

CHAPTER THREE

As their relationship deepened, Ava and Mason couldn't resist the attraction between them. They found themselves getting lost in steamy encounters whenever they had the chance, and Ava couldn't believe how amazing it felt to be with Mason.

He was passionate and attentive, and he made her feel beautiful and desired. Ava knew that she had found something special in Mason, and she couldn't wait to see where their relationship would take them. She didn't mind being with other men occasionally, but she never tried to push aside Mason's needs for hers. Instead, she focused on pleasing him as much as possible. She hoped that one day she might get pregnant from his sperm, but she figured if that time ever came, then so be it. It wouldn't change the fact that they were deeply in love.

When the couple went out to celebrate New Year's Eve, they headed back to his apartment instead of going to a club or bar. As the clock struck midnight, Ava kissed Mason passionately before making her way upstairs into the bedroom. Ava peeled off her tight-fitting dress before climbing onto the bed with her sexy new lover. They shared long, hot kisses before taking each other's clothes off until there was nothing left to cover up.

Mason climbed onto the bed and took Ava in his arms, and she instantly felt his hard cock pressing against her soft flesh.

"Fuck me!" she gasped, grabbing hold of his hands and pulling him towards her body. "Please... I need you inside me."

As she lay down on her back and spread her legs wide open for him, Mason slowly slid himself into her wet pussy. He grabbed her ass tightly while he rocked back and forth within her warm folds, feeling her clit rub against the tip of his penis. The intense sensations sent waves of pleasure radiating throughout Ava's entire body. She gripped the sheets beneath her with white knuckles as the ecstasy overtook her. After only a few minutes, she could barely breathe through the intensity of it all. But she was glad to have such a powerful orgasm—one that she didn't think she would ever experience again after her last relationship ended. And it felt even better when Mason reached down between her thighs, lifted her leg over his shoulder, and thrust deep inside her again.

She felt so loved that night, and she couldn't wait for their relationship to continue growing.

****

As their relationship continued to develop, Ava found herself falling deeper in love with Mason. She had never imagined finding someone so amazing at her age, but here she was in her mid-thirties already in a serious relationship with an incredibly handsome man who treated her like no one else had ever done before. Ava thought about the things they did together and wondered how long they could go without having sex before they became too bored.

One afternoon, Ava woke up from another dream about being naked and helpless, lying underneath her boyfriend as he forced his fingers and cock into her holes and abused her body in ways she'd always dreamed of, but never expected to actually experience. As she ran her hand across her smooth stomach, she realized that she must have been dreaming of Mason. Her body still felt sticky, and she looked down between her legs and saw her wetness seeping down her thigh. As she stood up off the bed and walked around the room barefooted, she noticed that her panties were stained with wetness. Ava was confused for a moment, wondering if this really meant that she was submissive enough to enjoy rough sexual encounters with her new lover. Then it hit her—she might be getting turned on while dreaming about what it would feel like for Mason to use her! It also dawned on her that perhaps her dreams weren't just fantasies after all...

Ava grabbed her phone out of her purse and pulled up her text messages. She smiled as she read the first few texts and found that they were all from Mason. She felt excited knowing that he wanted her again so soon and went straight to his apartment immediately.

As she let herself in through his front door, she could hear the shower running in his bathroom, which only made her hornier. The smell of soap mixed with Mason's cologne was intoxicating, but it was nothing compared with the smell coming from the bedroom, where a strong odor lingered. Ava grinned, remembering how much she liked smelling her boyfriend when they fucked.

She padded towards the bathroom to turn off the water as she continued peeking inside the room at everything there: a full-length mirror; stacks of DVDs and books; and framed photos of people whose names Ava couldn't recall at the moment.

Just as she got close to the bathroom door, Ava stopped dead in her tracks and covered her mouth in shock and surprise. There standing completely naked in the doorway was Mason, drying himself off with a towel that he had wrapped around his waist. He didn't see her yet because he was facing away from her. His beautiful back looked incredible—his firm shoulders were even more defined than before, and his perfectly chiseled six-pack looked perfect against the tight fit of his black boxer briefs. As Mason dried off, Ava could already tell that his body would look better with every passing day, and her pussy began to throb with excitement for him.

"Oh my god," she said aloud to herself. "I'm totally going to fuck your ass."

Mason heard her voice behind him and spun around to face her. His eyes lit up when he saw her, and he smiled.

"Hey!" he greeted happily as he took hold of her hand and pulled her into the shower. "What are you doing here?"

Ava gave him an impish smile while her heart beat wildly in her chest.

"I have a present for you," she replied with a sexy grin on her face.

As Mason stepped out of his underwear, Ava reached out and grabbed both sides of Mason's muscular thighs with one arm so she could lean over him to get closer to his cock. She ran her tongue along his shaft until it hardened to its full size under her wet touch, then moved down to lick it clean before starting to kiss and suck on the head of it. She slowly let her mouth slide lower towards the base of his hard member, taking it deep inside her throat. Mason moaned loudly as Ava bobbed her head back and forth, sucking and stroking his cock like a pro. Her warm, soft mouth felt amazing as she slurped and swallowed Mason's long, thick penis deeper and deeper with each stroke. When he finally got too sensitive in her mouth, he pushed her away. Then he stood upright against the wall and held his erect cock straight out in front of him.

Ava gazed up at him hungrily before crawling up between his legs and lowering herself onto the tip of his dick. She groaned deeply as she sank inch by inch onto him, letting her bare pussy grind into his hot skin beneath his pants while they made love right there in the bathroom. Once she had all eight inches buried deep inside her tightness, she sat down on top of him, straddling him, grinding her hips back and forth as she rocked them both forward and back in the shower.

Mason kissed Ava passionately while holding her body tightly against his. He could feel every part of their bodies moving together as they shared an intense orgasmic climax that left them both exhausted but satisfied. After making sure that Ava was okay, Mason dried off once again and headed for his bedroom to get dressed for work.

CHAPTER FOUR

As Ava and Mason's relationship continued to grow, they faced their fair share of challenges. They both had demanding careers, and it was difficult to find time for each other amidst their busy schedules.

In addition, they encountered some backlash from coworkers who didn't approve of their interracial relationship. Ava and Mason had to work hard to ignore the negativity and stay strong together.

But despite the challenges, Ava and Mason's love for each other only grew stronger. Their secretive sex life began getting more adventurous, with Mason becoming increasingly dominant in the bedroom. Every week he would show up at her place with new ideas or gifts—a collar he'd ordered online with a vibrating dildo attached; a video game console with games that allowed her to fuck her boyfriend as a female character instead of playing as a guy; a leather bondage suit which she found out about by accident when she stumbled upon one of his bags of clothing after he left town on business and brought home a few things for himself. Ava loved every present he gave her, and she felt lucky beyond belief knowing that someone so special cared enough to spoil her like this.

One evening, after they finished dinner and enjoyed an intense session of passionate lovemaking, Ava sat in front of the computer in their living room while Mason played videogames downstairs in the spare room. She typed away furiously at her keyboard until finally, after several hours of searching, she had everything ready to publish the next day. As soon as she hit the send button, Ava jumped out of her chair excitedly, then raced upstairs towards Mason's bedroom. He looked over his shoulder briefly from his screen before returning to his game as his girlfriend climbed into bed beside him.

"Hey baby!" Ava cooed playfully as she slid herself across his body.

Mason groaned in pleasure and pulled her close. His arms wrapped tightly around her body as he kissed down along her neck and throat and placed small kisses all the way down between her breasts. Then he moved lower and kissed along her smooth stomach, sucking and licking gently as he went. Ava moaned softly as her boyfriend kissed and teased her, feeling incredibly turned on by his affectionate attention. She closed her eyes and smiled contentedly, enjoying her boyfriend's gentle touch as he slowly made his way toward her swollen clit. Finally reaching its sweet spot, Mason started to suckle on it while rubbing his fingertips back and forth against it. He sucked it hard as he rubbed it at first, but then he began to use just his fingers to lightly rub against it too. The feel of Mason pleasuring her through her clothes drove Ava crazy with lust. Her juices began to trickle down her thighs, dripping onto the sheets below her.

Ava couldn't take the excitement anymore and pushed Mason off of her so she could sit up straight in bed.

"I can't wait any longer," she said breathlessly as she grabbed hold of Mason's shirt and pulled it off over his head. "Take your pants off now."

Mason obediently obeyed her order as his girlfriend crawled out from beneath his blankets and took hold of his zipper.

She was breathing heavily when she unzipped his pants and dragged them and his boxers down past his hips. As soon as they were completely gone, Ava got up out of the bed and ran downstairs to get some lubricant for their evening's activities. By the time she returned upstairs again, Mason had already shed the rest of his clothing, revealing a perfectly sculpted body that seemed to have been built specifically to pleasure women like Ava—hard muscle mass covered by dark brown skin tones, tan lines around every curve, flat stomach and washboard abs. His long cock looked even harder than usual dangling between his legs; all six inches standing proud and ready for action. Ava's pussy quivered as she walked towards him and kneeled between his legs on the edge of her bed.

Mason spread his legs wide open in anticipation as his new girlfriend slowly and seductively moved closer.

"Oh my god!" Ava moaned excitedly after taking one look at her boyfriend's cock in all its glory, pointing directly at her face. It wasn't big or anything, but it definitely stood out more prominently because of how much he was aroused at that moment, with a thin layer of precum dripping down its length. She wasted no time grabbing it with both hands to wrap her lips around it and began to lick the tip up and down. Mason let out a loud groan as Ava started to suck his hard shaft right away while continuing to kiss and suckle along his balls and pubic area too. After working her mouth up and down his entire length, she gave his crown one final suck before sliding her wet tongue downwards and running it up and down the underside of his throbbing erection. She used her fingers to lightly rub against the sensitive spot just beneath his glans which sent shockwaves of pleasure coursing through his body.

"That's so good," Mason said breathlessly as Ava worked his thick dick like a pro. "You're going to make me cum."

Ava looked into Mason's eyes as she wrapped her hand around his cock and jerked him off furiously, faster than ever before. Every thrust inside her warm mouth made her hotter than she already was, and she knew that soon she would feel that familiar surge that meant she could give him a little something extra if he wanted it—something that only she was capable of giving him that nobody else had yet. Ava slipped two of her fingers back into her wet pussy until they were coated in her own juices, then held them in front of Mason's face as she continued sucking his stiff rod.

"Put your finger in my ass baby!" Ava begged. "I want you to put it in my tight little asshole!"

Mason smiled as he watched his girl-friend get even more turned on by the dirty talk. He didn't think twice about do-ing what she asked. It wasn't the first time he'd pleasured Ava with a couple of fingers up there, but this time felt different some-how because he really needed to cum right now; he couldn't hold out much longer without letting go. As soon as he pushed a single fingertip into her puckered anus, Ava cried out and sucked hard onto Ma-son's penis harder than before. Her tiny body shook all over and her breathing be-came ragged and fast. She came hard and violently and squirted several shots of her sweet nectar all over Mason's chest and belly while still jerking his cock furiously between her lips. After coming down from her orgasmic high, Ava slid down beside

Mason to lick up every last drop of their love making together, then kissed him deeply for a long while afterwards, tasting the saltiness of her sweat mixed with his precum as it dribbled off her chin.

"That was the most amazing thing I have ever seen," Mason whispered lovingly as he gazed into his girlfriend's beautiful eyes.

CHAPTER FIVE

As Ava and Mason looked towards the future, they knew that they had found something special in each other.

Mason made sure that he never missed any opportunities to show Ava how important she was to him or that she had anything to be ashamed of. They talked openly about everything, including Ava's history with men, and made sure to share those stories during sex to ensure that both of them got enjoyment from them. This included details about one night when Ava was having a bad day at work—a time where some of the women who worked there gave her a hard time because she wasn't like them—until she decided to let the situation turn sexual. In addition, she told Mason about the time when her cousin hit on her while her family was visiting her hometown; how she played along until she started kissing her and touching her body; how it turned into a real-life fantasy come true; and then eventually led to an intense lesbian affair that left her wanting more.

"I always wondered if I would've done things differently in my past life," Ava said as she wrapped her arms around her boyfriend's neck. "If I'd been born as a man instead of a woman."

"No way," Mason replied firmly as he held his girlfriend close to him. "You're perfect just the way you are. There's nothing wrong with you or what happened before, so don't ever think like that again. You did absolutely nothing wrong, baby!"

Mason loved being with Ava, and the thought of living without her seemed completely unthinkable now. He couldn't imagine another person besides Ava for the rest of his life. So for their anniversary together, he took her out for their biggest celebration yet: dinner and dancing in downtown Detroit. Mason surprised his girlfriend by picking up a special outfit for her to wear: a long flowing red dress that skimmed down to the tops of her knees but stopped above her ankles. The dress was paired with black high heels which matched perfectly with the black purse she wore over her shoulder that also carried a pair of matching earrings she bought that morning. On top of all this, Ava was wearing makeup too—her dark brown hair tied back into two French braids that framed her beautiful face, and a touch of lipstick added just the right amount of pep into her look. They were getting ready at home when Mason's phone rang and he stepped away from them both into the kitchen to answer it.

"It's your dad," he said excitedly after hanging up the call. "He wants me to meet him at one of our favorite bars in town tonight."

"Really?" Ava asked playfully as she continued admiring herself in the mirror. "So you won't be able to come pick me up for work tomorrow? It will suck having to walk in on my own."

"Oh, come on," Mason teased, smacking her on the butt while smiling. "I wouldn't miss seeing you looking so good for anything! Besides, I have an idea how we can make sure you don't get fired you happened to arrive late anyway."

"What do you mean?" Ava asked curiously as Mason picked up her keys and tossed them over his shoulder onto the bed where she sat.

Then he quickly dropped to his knees and took hold of his girlfriend's tiny feet. He kissed her soft toes and worked his way up to her ankles before moving to her shapely calves. She watched with delight as he moved up to her thighs then slowly made his way up towards her panties until finally coming to a stop directly above the heart shaped tattoo located just above the crotch line between her legs. Her pussy was already dripping wet, and a slight quiver ran down her spine when she realized what he had planned next. Ava wasn't going anywhere without letting her boyfriend lick her sweet little clit first, however.

Mason lifted Ava's dress up around her hips to reveal her white cotton panties which were now completely drenched in anticipation. The front of her underwear was decorated with pink flowers and butterflies along with some other drawings that looked like they were drawn by hand instead of being printed by a machine. Mason pressed his face into them briefly before opening them wide open so that he could reach inside the front panel. His tongue immediately found its way into her tight, hot box as she held onto the bed handle behind her for dear life. Mason moaned out loud as he tasted every inch of his girlfriend's vagina for the very first time, relishing it as much as she did.

"Oh my god!" Ava screamed after getting off from watching him eat her out while rubbing herself all over the place.

Mason got back on his knees and pulled Ava's soaked panties down past her knees to join the rest of her clothes on the floor. Then he took hold of her slender ankles and wrapped them over each shoulder before bringing his head up close to hers again to start kissing her softly. As their tongues danced together, Ava couldn't help but feel another climax building within her body, and before long, she felt the familiar surge of pleasure wash over her as her legs started to shake uncontrollably—something only one person had ever been able to do this to her: Mason, her boyfriend. Ava leaned forward against the door with her arms crossed beneath her breasts, still shaking as a few more squirts of her girl cum fell down onto her shirt.

When Mason finally released Ava's feet from his grasp, he stood up straight once again with a huge smile on his face.

"Well?" Ava asked breathlessly. "Do you have something else planned? Because I'm ready right now."

Mason kissed his girlfriend deeply then picked her up in his strong arms and carried her towards the bedroom where they both jumped into bed for some extra-special post-workout loving. When they were finished having sex, they made sure not to waste any time showering and getting dressed before going out to celebrate their anniversary. The bar they ended up at was nothing too fancy or exclusive; just an old fashioned neighborhood joint that served cheap beer and shots all night long. They sat outside around a small fire pit under the stars which allowed them to be surrounded by people of all ages dancing to music that would've sounded like classic rock if it weren't being played by today's hipster bands instead of the classics.

Ava smiled widely as she watched Mason dance beside her with his arm around her shoulders as she clung tightly to his waist while keeping her legs together so that he couldn't see what she looked so excited about inside her tight fitting dress. He led her around on the dance floor, occasionally spinning her away from him so that he could get a better look down the front of her outfit, but eventually he turned her back and spun her back toward him again. She felt him put his hand on the back of her neck from behind and kiss the nape of her exposed shoulder blade before taking hold of her left hand and guiding her closer until their bodies touched.

"You're making me hot," Ava whispered when Mason kissed her earlobe as she stood in place with one foot in front of the other—her best effort at holding herself upright against his weight while dancing with him.

"I know how much you love feeling my hard cock against your soft skin," he replied with a naughty grin on his face. "Don't tell me you don't feel that?"

Mason slowly started rubbing himself through his pants, causing Ava to smile wide as a blush crept up onto her cheeks. Her boyfriend had seen this expression come over her face many times before, and there was no mistaking why: it was because of something deep within her body that was only brought out during sex. His hard-on rubbed against her thigh and caused her pussy lips to start swelling once again and leak some more of the sweet nectar that dripped out of them.

Ava's eyes went wide with excitement after she realized what he was trying to do. It wasn't every day she got to enjoy an orgasm in public; however, if she let go of Mason's arm she knew she would fall right on her ass if she tried anything too fancy. So instead, she reached for his wrist and placed his hand on top of hers, intertwining their fingers together tightly so they would both be able to experience everything together without getting into trouble. When Mason did the same thing by placing his hand between her breasts where she could feel its warmth under her dress, all hell broke loose inside her. She squeezed him back even harder than before as another climax built inside her before bursting forth with force. She moaned loudly as a floodgate opened up inside her which left her unable to control any sounds coming from her mouth other than the loudest purring noise ever heard in history.

When Ava finally caught her breath again, she looked up at Mason who just stared at her in disbelief as he watched her squirm against his touch. Then he kissed her deeply on the cheek while holding her close in his arms. He still didn't seem entirely sure that this was happening or how he should act around it.

CHAPTER SIX

Ava was dreaming about three strangers. She led the strangers down the hall past all of her neighbors' rooms until they reached hers, where they stood together in front of her door. One man pushed his crotch against Ava's butt as he pressed his body up close to hers, while another did the exact same thing on her other side. Ava smiled nervously at them before pulling open her own door and stepping inside. Then she quickly closed the door behind her and hurriedly tried to get out of her clothes while standing naked in the middle of the room with her hands over her breasts and ass. All three men were smiling as they looked down upon the terrified woman they'd trapped between them in her tiny apartment. The one with his hand stuck in his fly couldn't hide how much bigger than her he was. He grinned as he took hold of her wrists to pin them above her head then squeezed hard enough to bruise them slightly with each twist. His grin widened further as he ripped off her skirt, along with her thong underneath it. Ava cried out in pain as she felt her underwear rip off, making it impossible to cover herself up any longer.

The man continued to laugh at Ava's reaction while unzipping his zipper, releasing the largest erect cock Ava had ever seen. It was a little over ten inches long and extremely thick—with veins bulging all over the shaft. She shivered with excitement as the guy grabbed his cock and stroked it slowly while staring at her face intently. She watched him stroke himself back and forth and thought about how amazing it would be if that monster of a dick ended up buried inside her tight pussy. The two other guys kept her pinned against the wall with their bodies too, but they didn't seem to care; they just wanted to watch. She noticed that one of them had moved closer so that he could take in her body as well. When she finally caught on, she stopped trying to fight them and started doing exactly what they wanted instead. Her breathing became erratic again when she realized what was happening and what was going to happen next. Ava began grinding her hips and ass into his groin which made his erection throb even harder before grabbing hold of the waistband of his pants once more. With a quick yank, she pulled the pants down to his knees revealing his hairy legs along with an enormous pair of balls dangling below them. Then she turned around to kneel in front of him in only her thong. The man stepped back to give her space as he placed one hand flat on her back to keep her close while the other held onto the hem of her thong by her ankle. He gave her taint a playful squeeze while rubbing his swollen member through his boxers against the top of her smooth bare butt cheeks before quickly pushing it through the hole in her panties. Ava cried out at first, but then let out a loud moan of pleasure when the stranger's fat cock slid right up her dripping slit without any hesitation. As soon as the tip bumped up against her pussy lips, Ava felt a surge of ecstasy course through her body.

"Oh my god!" She gasped. "You feel so good! It feels amazing!"

The man slowly pressed forward until the head of his penis was resting against her slick outer labia—still fully contained within her tight pink folds—and he started rocking back and forth. The pressure was building inside of him rapidly now that he had finally gotten inside of her and he couldn't wait much longer to push deep inside this sexy black girl he had been eyeing all day long. He gripped her hips firmly with both hands as she squirmed beneath him, keeping her from moving too far away. When she reached for his shoulders with both arms, she wasn't trying to get him off; she just needed some more leverage to move with his thrusts while trying to grind her clit into his pelvis with every downstroke. Ava began humping her crotch hard into the base of his shaft like a madwoman; the slapping sound of their bodies colliding filled the air around them. Every time he pulled back slightly, Ava would try to climb up on top of him in order to keep grinding herself onto him, but he held on tightly and continued holding her in place. He wanted to make sure that everything happened at exactly the same pace, even if it meant giving in to his own urges and forcing her to take control over how they fucked each other instead. The man knew that Ava wouldn't be able to handle taking his entire monster dick inside her pussy so soon after cumming earlier that evening, but as he moved deeper and harder between her legs, the thought excited him beyond belief. His erection grew stiffer than ever before as he teased himself by letting out soft moans which echoed through the small apartment as well as the rest of the complex.

"Oh god! Oh fuck! Fuck yeah!" The man grunted.

"Oh god!" She whimpered.

The room was spinning again. The feeling of her tight wet lips surrounding his thick shaft made his knees buckle a little and he almost lost his balance completely, causing him to drop his grip on her hips to grab hold of her body for support. Then a loud slap erupted behind her, making both of them jump a bit; then there were two more quick, hard smacks followed by another louder one—and yet more—until she felt someone's hand wrap firmly around her neck. Another guy stood directly beside her now with an equally monstrous penis bulging against the front of his pants, eager to finally get inside this woman who had been taunting him all day long from afar. He reached around her head with one hand while grabbing the waistband of her panties and yanked them down to her ankles in the next second while the first man held her firmly in place and kept pounding away into her from above. Ava couldn't believe how easily he pulled down those sexy black thong pant-ies and how much bigger his cock looked compared to her lover's already. The stranger grabbed onto Ava's thighs like handles and started lifting up and pushing his groin deeper up inside her cunt, until he could feel his balls pressed up against his belly button as well as his entire cock buried inside her tight walls.

"Oh shit! I'm going to cum!" He cried out. "Oh fuck yes! So fucking good!"

He gave her taint another playful squeeze before giving it a firm tug back to-wards him. Ava screamed when she felt the pressure build between her legs once again; it only took seconds before it ex-ploded through every single inch of her body: It hit her toes and then the tips of her fingers on the other side of the wall and went straight through the wall itself without missing a beat, right through all three men standing on either side of her and then through the other apartments where anyone else might have been listening or watching too, exploding outside the building altogether and making quite a racket. The man continued to slam his hips forward while holding tightly to her body, not letting go of her waist. When he heard someone walk across the hallway to see what was happening, he just slammed himself as deep as possible in order to drown them all out with his loud grunts—and even louder screams—of ecstasy. All four bodies shuddered at once from the forceful impact—three that belonged to strangers along with their two lovers—and everyone groaned loudly with satisfaction after coming together for the very first time tonight. After that Ava woke up

CHAPTER SEVEN

As they settled into their new home, Ava and Mason knew that they had found something rare and precious in each other. They were committed to building a life together and to supporting each other in all their endeavors.

They knew that there would be challenges ahead, but they were ready to face them as a team. They were grateful for the love and support they had for each other, and they knew that they were meant to be together. For as long as they both lived, the two people who loved one another most deeply shared an unbreakable bond that could never be broken by anything except death. As Ava slept peacefully next to her man on the night of their anniversary, she thought about how happy she was to have finally found him. She realized how blessed she truly was because she wasn't alone anymore; she had her best friend here beside her now to help her make it through this tough time in her life—and whatever else came down the line. Her life couldn't get much better than it already did; she wouldn't trade it for anything else in the world. She didn't care what happened tomorrow or if everything changed between them, so long as he remained close enough for her to feel safe and protected by his presence right there with her every step of the way. Even though some parts of their relationship still felt unfinished, she believed that things were going to work out exactly as they were supposed to no matter how far away they went from each other physically: It was always good being near someone you cared about.

***